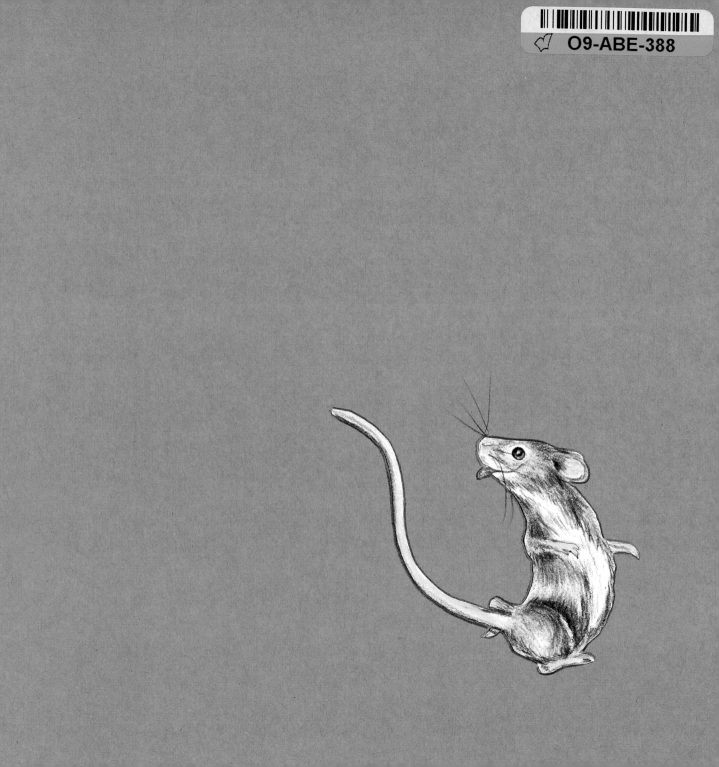

For Mom and Dad

10 9 8 7 6 5 4 3 2 1

First Edition

Published by Lark Books,
A Division of Sterling Publishing Co., Inc.
387 Park Avenue South, New York, NY 10016

© 2008, Elizabeth Zechel

Distributed in Canada by Sterling Publishing,
c/o Canadian Manda Group, 165 Dufferin Street
Toronto, Ontario, Canada M6K 3H6

Distributed in the United Kingdom by GMC Distribution Services,
Castle Place, 166 High Street, Lewes, East Sussex, England BN7 1XU

Distributed in Australia by Capricorn Link (Australia) Pty Ltd.,
P.O. Box 704, Windsor, NSW 2756 Australia

If you have questions or comments about this book, please contact:
Lark Books
67 Broadway
Asheville, NC 28801
828-253-0467

Manufactured in China

ISBN 13: 978-1-60059-266-9

For information about custom editions, special sales, premium and corporate purchases, please contact Sterling Special Sales Department at 800-805-5489 or specialsales@sterlingpub.com.

Is There a MOUSE in the Baby's Room?

Elizabeth Zechel

LARK BOOKS

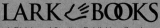

A Division of Sterling Publishing Co., Inc.,
New York / London

Here is a baby.
(Isn't he adorable?!)

He has wonderful parents who love him very much.

They feed him when he's hungry.

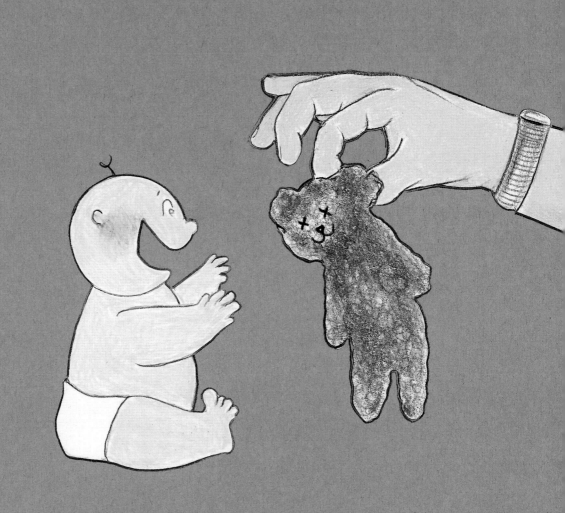

They play with him when he's bored.

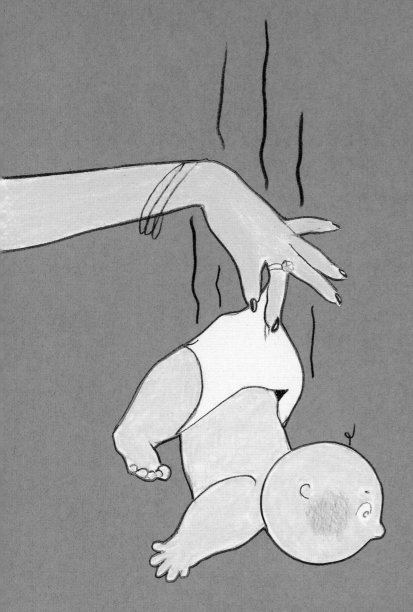

They change his diaper when he's stinky.

And they put him to bed when he's sleepy.

squeak!
squeak!

One day, Mom thought she heard
a strange noise coming from
the baby's room.

In fact, it was coming from…

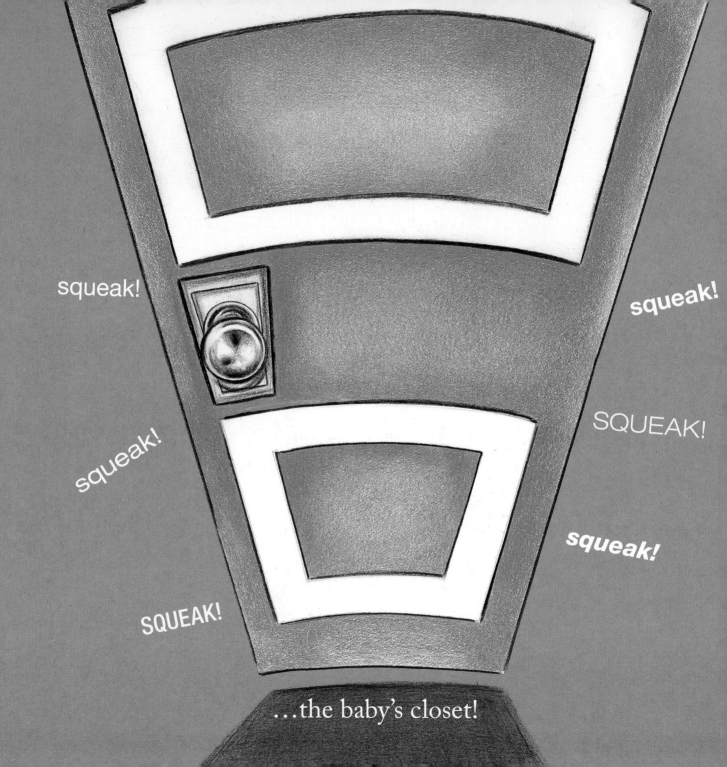

"Did you hear something, dear?" said Mom.

"No, dear. Why? Did
you hear something?"
said Dad.

"I thought I heard something in the
baby's room," said Mom.

"The baby's room?" said Dad. "Well, that's strange. What did it sound like?"

"It sounded like a mouse in the baby's room," said Mom.

"A mouse in the baby's room?" said Dad.
That's just silly. There isn't a mouse in the baby's room!"

"Well, I really, truly thought it sounded like a mouse in the baby's room," said Mom.

"If there was a mouse in the baby's room," said Dad,
"we'd know if there was a mouse in the baby's room."

"Are you sure you don't think there's a mouse in the baby's room?" said Mom.

VROO

"I'm positively, absolutely positive there isn't a mouse in the baby's room," said Dad.

"What was that???" said Mom and Dad together. And they rushed into the baby's room.

"Oh look," said Mom, "the baby fell out of the crib. We'll just put him back to bed. Poor little thing."

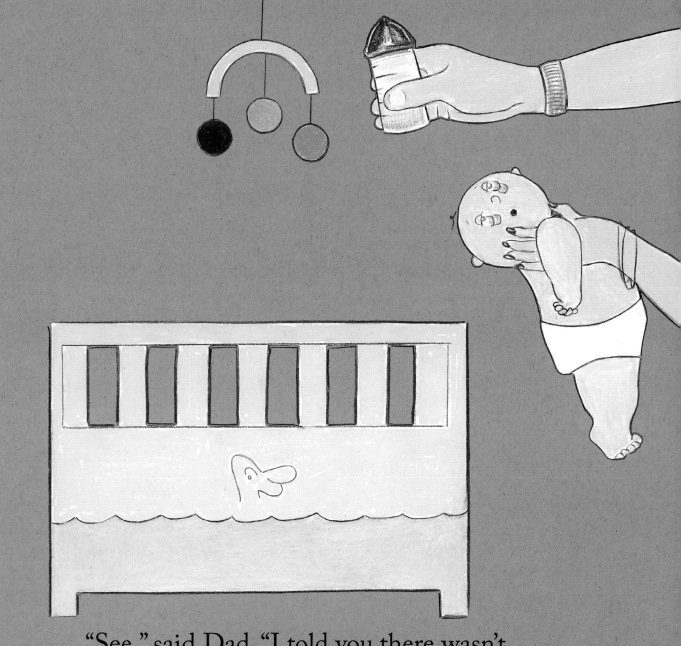

"See," said Dad, "I told you there wasn't a mouse in the baby's room."

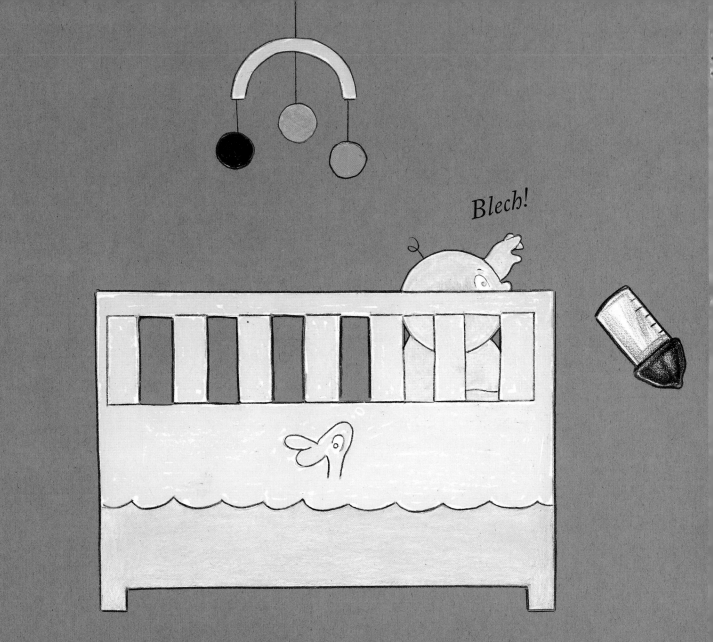

"Good night," said Mom.
"Good night," said Dad.

zzzzzzz